PALANQUIN

OPHELIA HOUSE
ASSASSINS

OPHELIA HOUSE

ASSASSINS

ORIGINAL ARTWORK

ANDREW L. WILLIS

CREATED AND WRITTEN

CARLTON L. SAMPSON
COVER DESIGN, BALLOONS, PAGE LAYOUT

Palanquin

THE COLONIAL HOTEL

"PO LYN LEE "OPHELIA HOUSE" EPISODE 4 "FIRST FRIDAY" PAGE 28.

- 15 -

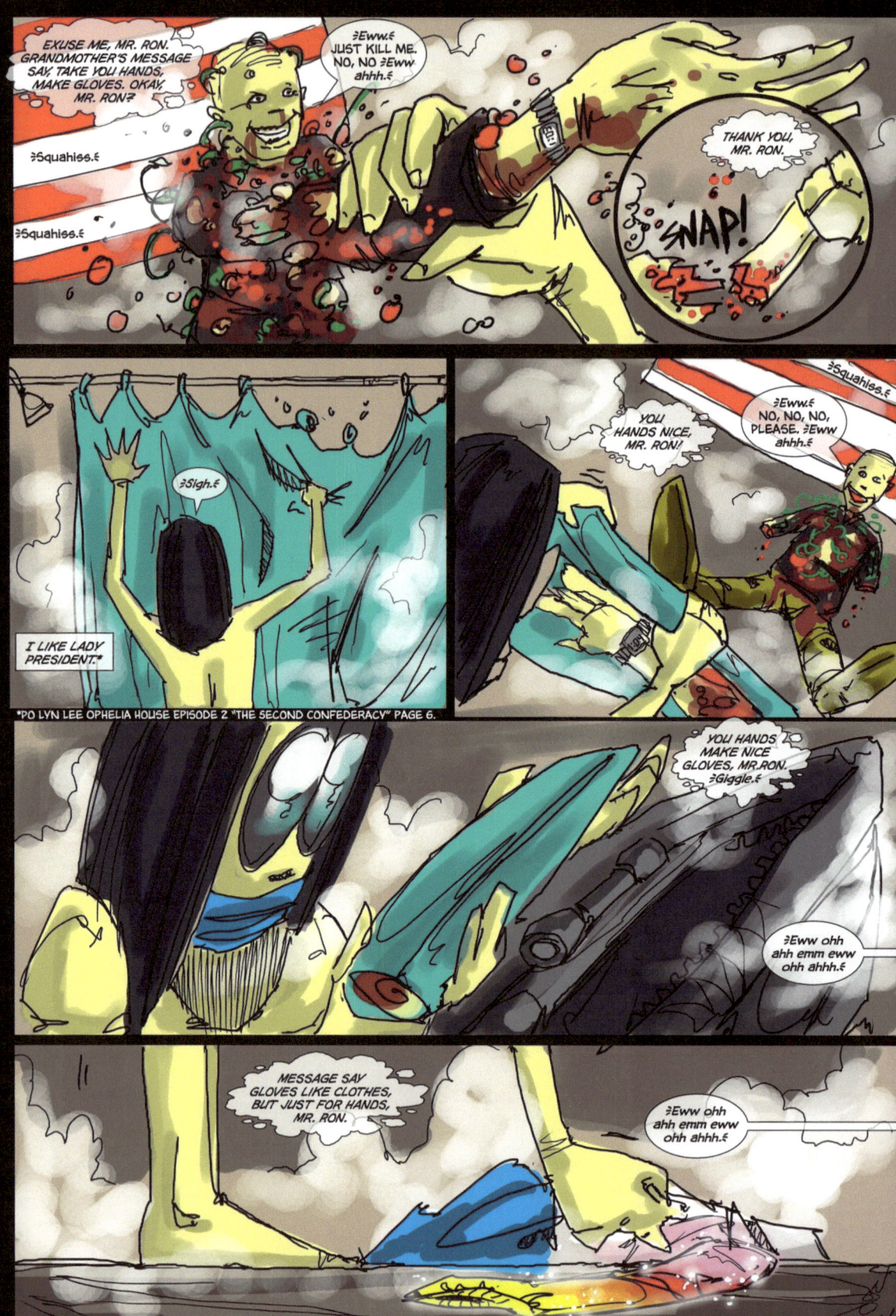

*PO LYN LEE OPHELIA HOUSE EPISODE 2 "THE SECOND CONFEDERACY" PAGE 6.

*PO LYN LEE OPHELIA HOUSE EPISODE 1 "THE S.I.C. JOB" PAGE 24.

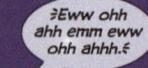

*PO LYN LEE "OPHELIA HOUSE" EPISODE 3 "LADY LIBERTY" PAGE 2.

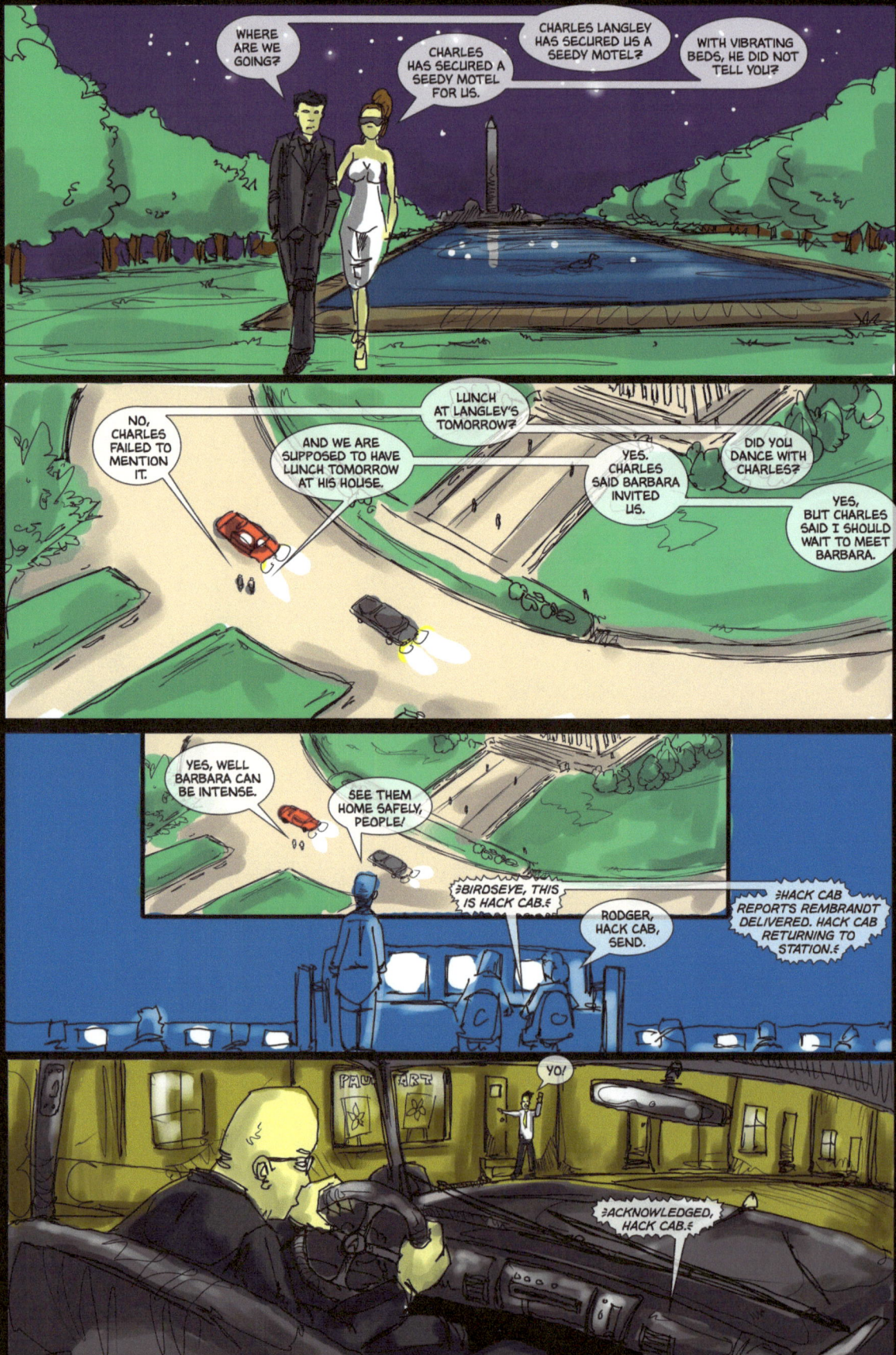

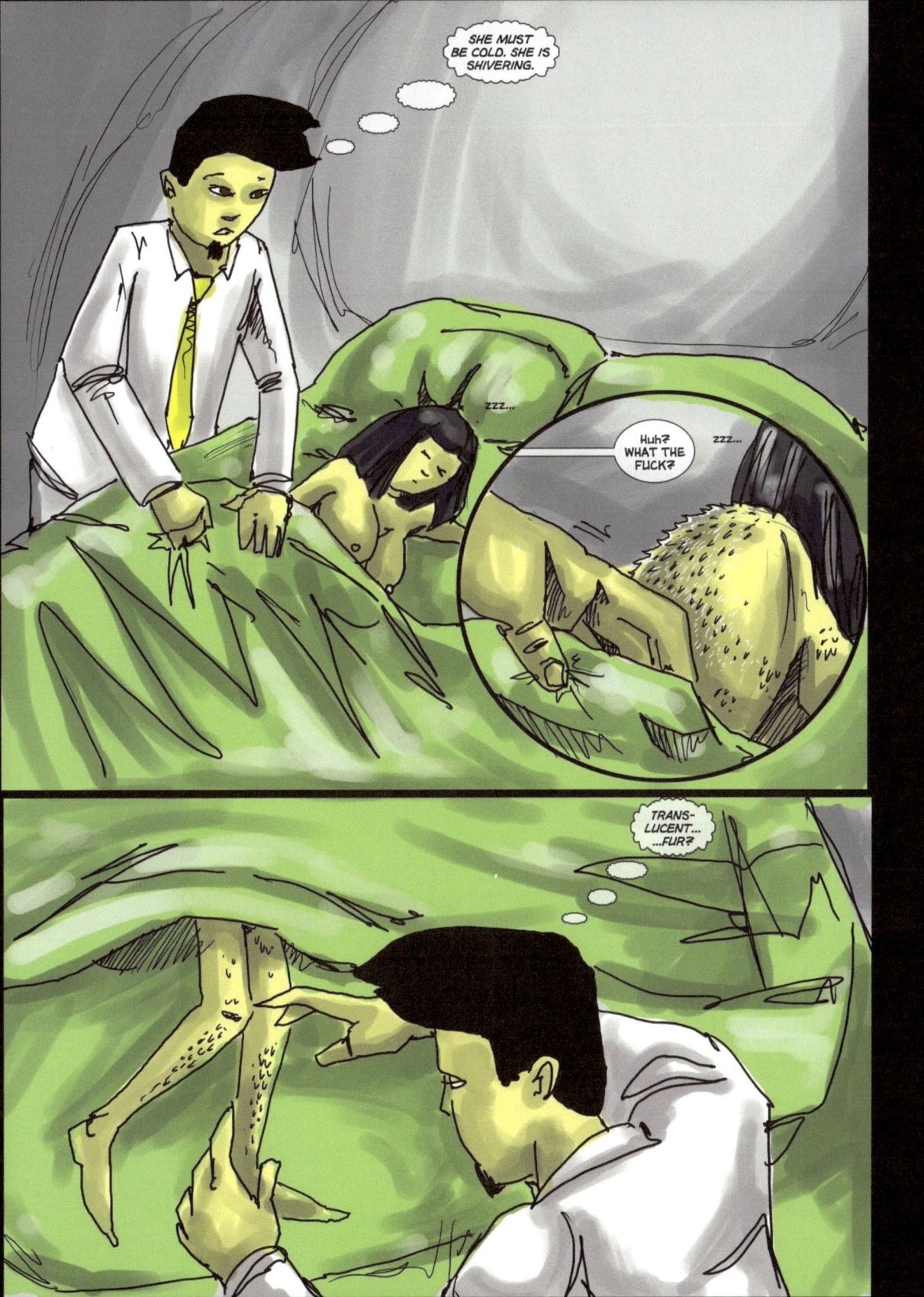

PO LYN LEE
OPHELIA HOUSE
NEXT ISSUE

"SHADOW OF THE HIVE"

IT IS THE MORNING AFTER. MARY-ANNE CURTIS ARIVES EARLY TOWED BY MARTHA RANDOLPH CURTIS THE SECOND'S ENTOURAGE TO CATCH PO COLORFULLY UNVEILED AND NAPPING IN THE NUDE. GAIL PALMER INSISTS PAUL STEWART AND PO NOT ONLY COURT BUT ALSO SEE TO IT THERE IS A WEDDING. PAUL STEWART LEARNS ONE OF LIFE'S BIGGEST LESSONS AND REALIZES HE IS TOO LATE FOR BREWSTER'S ART CLASS.

CARLTON L. SAMPSON

POET, GRAPHIC NOVELL AUTHOR
CARLTON@POLYNLEE.COM
OTHER WORK AVAILABLE AT:
WWW.PHASCISTCLOWNS.COM

ANDREW L. WILLIS

AKA, THIOBIS THE ARTIST
FINE ART, SCULPTURE, ANIMATION,
MUSIC, AND WRITTEN.
ANDREW@POLYNLEE.COM
OTHER WORK AVAILABLE AT:
WWW.WAOOBAKEARTWORK.COM

THE RANDOLPH CAVERNS

IT IS THE MORNING AFTER. MARY-ANNE CURTIS ARRIVES EARLY TOWED
BY MARTHA RANDOLPH CURTIS THE SECOND'S ENTOURAGE TO CATCH PO
COLORFULLY UNVEILED AND NAPPING IN THE NUDE. GAIL PALMER INSISTS
PAUL STEWART AND PO NOT ONLY COURT BUT ALSO SEE TO IT THERE IS A
WEDDING. PAUL STEWART LEARNS ONE OF LIFE'S BIGGEST LESSONS AND
REALIZES HE IS TOO LATE FOR BREWSTER ANDREW'S ART CLASS.

NEXT ISSUE

WWW.POLYNLEE.COM